# TOMMY DONBAVAND'S FUNNY  SHORTS

# INVASION OF BADGER'S BOTTOM

## WRITTEN BY TOMMY DONBAVAND
## ILLUSTRATED BY CLAUDIA SOUZA

EDGE
FRANKLIN WATTS

LONDON·SYDNEY

Franklin Watts
First published in Great Britain in 2017 by The Watts Publishing Group

Credits
Executive Editor: Adrian Cole
Design Manager: Peter Scoulding
Cover Designer: Cathryn Gilbert
Illustrations: Claudia Souza

HB ISBN 978 1 4451 5382 7
PB ISBN 978 1 4451 5384 1
Library ebook ISBN 978 1 4451 5383 4

Printed in China.

Franklin Watts
An imprint of
Hachette Children's Group
Part of The Watts Publishing Group
Carmelite House
50 Victoria Embankment
London EC4Y 0DZ

An Hachette UK Company
www.hachette.co.uk

www.franklinwatts.co.uk

# Contents

Chapter One: Invaders          6

Chapter Two: Identify          16

Chapter Three: Insults         26

Chapter Four: Interruption     38

Chapter Five: Idea             47

Chapter Six: Incoming!         57

# CHAPTER ONE
## Invaders

The sky fizzed with electricity as a
shimmering spaceship flew down through
thick clouds. It was shaped like a strange
gremlin, built from chunky computer pixels.
The spaceship cast a creepy glow over the
open-mouthed people watching from the
ground.

They stared in horror as this lone UFO was
joined by a second spaceship — identical
to the first. Then another, and another.

Within moments, the sky was filled with spaceships, all arranged in a single long line. Then, they began moving a metre at a time. Sideways.

The alien invasion of Earth had begun.

As the farthest ship reached the horizon, the entire squadron suddenly plunged down towards the ground. Many people screamed and ran. Others stood rooted to the spot.

But, almost as quickly as they had started their descent, the invaders stopped — just thirty metres or so below their original position — and then they began to shuffle back towards the city. Back to where they had first appeared.

This unexpected drop had allowed yet another row of spacecraft — more duplicates — to appear from the heavy cloud cover. Now there were twice as many invaders as before!

As the ships were closer to the ground,

people could now hear an angry, repetitive noise coming from each one.

UN! UN! UN! UN! UN! UN! UN! UN! UN!

Those watching couldn't just hear the noise. They could feel it, pounding inside their bodies, slamming against their hearts and making their brains vibrate like jelly.

UN! UN! UN! UN! UN! UN! UN! UN! UN!

Then the two rows of ships dropped again, allowing a third line to appear. The squadron started back towards the coast in the same motion as before.

UN! UN! UN! UN! UN! UN! UN! UN! UN!

By the time they reached the ground, there would be enough alien invaders to—

"Scratch my nose!"

Jamie Ross hit pause on his tablet and looked up to find his cousin standing over him, her shadow blocking the warm summer sunlight. "What?"

"Can you scratch my nose?" asked Megan, leaning down and jutting her face in his direction. "I've got an itch, but there's paint all over my hands, so I can't do it myself."

Jamie blinked. "Then, wash your hands."

"I can't!" moaned Megan. "Well, I can — obviously. But, by the time I go inside and do that, the itch will have gone!"

"Isn't that a good thing?"

"No!" exclaimed Megan. "I enjoy having

my itches scratched, and I don't like them to think they've got away with it..."

With a sigh, Jamie reached out and began to scratch his cousin's nose with the end of his finger.

"No, not there!" said Megan, swivelling her eyes down and trying to look at the spot Jamie was working on. It made her look like a cross-eyed pug.

"The other side. Up a bit. Bit more.

That's it! Now I can get back to my picture."

Jamie glanced over at the large sheet of card standing near the garden fence. Megan was halfway through a painting of a city skyline at sunset. He had to admit that it looked amazing, but it wasn't the skyline of Badger's Bottom — the sleepy town where they lived. It was a mixture of lots of famous landmarks: the Statue of Liberty, the Eiffel Tower, Sydney Opera House, Big Ben.

"You know you've got paint all over you, right?" said Jamie.

"So? At least I'm doing something creative. You're just playing some stupid ancient computer game."

"Space Invaders isn't stupid!" Jamie
retorted, starting the level again. "It's
brilliant!"

Megan glanced down at the blocky alien craft on the screen. "But it's years old..."

"It's a classic!"

"You just have to shoot the same ships over and over again..."

"That's the challenge!"

"The graphics are terrible..."

Jamie grinned. "Not if you use your imagination, like I do."

"No," Megan insisted. "They're terrible. Real UFOs don't look like that."

Jamie frowned. "And how would you know?"

The colour had drained from Megan's face (apart from all of the paint). "Because there's one in the sky right behind you!"

# CHAPTER TWO
## Identify

The spaceship landed in the back garden, and after the jets of steam and flashing lights had stopped, three aliens emerged. One stepped forwards.

"Take us to your leader!"

The alien's voice sounded metallic — like someone was talking through the whirring blades of a spinning fan.

The ray gun it was holding looked like a cheap plastic toy, but Jamie and Megan

were in little doubt that the weapon could hurt them, and possibly even blast them into clouds of dust.

That would totally ruin the summer holidays.

The spaceship didn't look like the ones in Jamie's game app. This one was sleek, silver and disc-shaped.

The aliens had grey skin, and wore identical blue jumpsuits made from some strange, other-worldly material. The creatures each had a single, large eye in the middle of their oversized spotty bald heads, and thin, lipless mouths. They looked a lot like Jamie's maths teacher trying to solve a particularly tough equation.

The aliens were terrifying, or they would have been, had they been more than 30 centimetres tall.

"I said, take us to your leader!" the alien in the centre of the trio demanded in his screechy, high-pitched voice.

"Who do you mean?" asked Megan.

The alien blinked slowly, then opened his single eye wide, his jet black eyeball staring. "Your leader!" he repeated. "Take us to him."

"Or her," added another of the creatures. His voice was even squeakier than the first. "There's no reason that this planet would have a male-dominated society."

The middle alien sighed. It sounded like someone gargling with a handful of staples. "All right..." he groaned. "Take us to your leader — he or she."

"What if they've got more than two genders?" asked the third being. His voice was slightly deeper, and croaky too. The central alien, clearly the one in charge, rubbed at his forehead with the handle of his gun. "Look, there's nothing in the research to say they've got more than two genders!"

"How would you know?" demanded the older alien. "You didn't even read the file."

"Enough!" barked the commander.

"How come you can speak English?" Megan interrupted.

The two outer aliens turned to face their captain. He scowled — which wasn't an easy expression to achieve without any eyebrows.

"How should I know?" he spat. "I didn't
even want to come on this stupid mission. I
was quite happy looking after Major Pain's
throne. But, oh no... You two had to go and

tell him that there was a planet out there we hadn't conquered yet. And now here we are, on a crazy alien world, insisting two giants take us to visit whoever's in charge."

"Major Pain?" questioned Jamie. "Who's that?"

The alien leader squinted at him. "I'll tell you, but would you mind sitting down first? Or at least kneeling? I'm getting a crick in the back of my neck from looking up at you. I had no idea you were going to be so tall."

"You would have known if you'd bothered to read the mission details like you were supposed to," muttered his older companion.

"Not this, again!"

The kids both sat cross-legged on the grass. "Go on," urged Jamie. "You were about to tell us about this Major Pain..."

"Wait!" cried the younger alien. "Why tell them when we can show them?" And with that, he sprinted back inside the coffee-table sized flying saucer.

"My name's Megan," said Megan with a smile. "This is my cousin, Jamie."

"That was Bigg, and I am Smellie," announced the older of the two remaining creatures. "Our brave and glorious commander here is Faart. We're from the planet Soolin."

"Really?" said Jamie, sniggering.

"Did I miss anything?" said Bigg, returning

from the ship.

"No, not much," said Megan with a chuckle.

"Good, because I've got something scary

to show you..."

# CHAPTER THREE
## Insults

Bigg produced what appeared to be some kind of tablet made from a single sheet of shimmering glass. "I haven't finished editing this video yet, so it has still got some mistakes in…"

Faart sighed heavily. "Just show them the film…"

"OK!" Bigg slid his palm across the sheet of glass and a collection of icons appeared. He extended one of the three fingers on his right hand, and used it to tap on a small picture of a movie clip. A video file opened. He held the tablet flat, and an image projected from the surface.

The movie started, showing a large and richly decorated room. The floor was covered in plush purple carpet, and four large golden pillars stretched up towards a distant ceiling. Paintings of an alien hung on the sparkling gold walls. The figure was wearing a military uniform, decorated almost completely in shiny medals.

In some pictures, the figure was saluting, in others the alien was sitting astride what looked like a fat pink camel. In all of them, he looked as though he had just bitten into a burger with no pickles, and found nothing but pickles. He did not look happy at all.

The camera zoomed in to focus on a raised platform at the end of the room, on which sat a gleaming white and red throne. A hidden door opened in the wall, and a well-dressed alien stepped into the room. It was the grumpy alien from the room's many portraits.

"That's Major Pain!" hissed Bigg. "He's our leader!"

On screen, Major Pain stopped beside his throne and glared down at it, his face twisting into a picture of rage.

"Faart!" he bellowed at the top of his voice. "Get in here!"

Faart zoomed into the room.

"Why hasn't my throne been brushed today?" demanded Major Pain.

"I, er ... I was just getting round to it, oh glorious ruler," Faart replied. "I'll do it now!"

"See that you do!" growled Pain. "I have to deliver updated battle plans to my generals for the war on Baxendale 9. I want it brushed to a perfect shine by the time I get back!"

Faart bowed deeply. "Yes, your amazing majestic nastiness!"

As Major Pain strode out of the room, Faart produced what looked like a large toothbrush, and a long tube. Working quickly, he squeezed some thick goo out of the tube, covering the brush's bristles. He then proceeded to brush the throne.

"Hang on," said Megan. "Why are you treating the throne as if it's made of teeth?"

"Because it is," explained Bigg. "Major Pain likes to sit on a throne made from the teeth of his enemies."

"And it takes me hours every day to brush the thing!" Faart groaned. "It's my job."

"But, I thought you were in the army or something," said Jamie. "Isn't that why you're here, leading the invasion?"

"Nooooo," said Smellie with a chuckle. "The entire Soolin army is busy conquering other worlds and star systems. There were no warriors left for Major Pain to send to Earth."

"I spotted a way we could get off Soolin

for a bit of a holiday," Bigg said with a strange sideways wink. "So, I told him all about you, and volunteered us for the mission."

"You're not a soldier?" asked Jamie.

Bigg shook his head. "I work in the palace kitchens putting the toppings on Major Pain's cakes, and Smellie is his chief gardener."

"I look after the lawns," said the older alien. "It's hard work. I needed a break."

"So he went along with black-hole brain here and signed us up to be the first wave to invade your planet," finished Faart. "And here we are…"

"Ooh, we're coming up to the funny bit!" said Bigg, pointing at the movie.

The group watched as Major Pain stomped back into the room. He was reading from a glass screen of his own. He seemed to be in an even darker mood than he had been earlier, if such a thing was possible.

"I hope you're finished, Faart!" he rumbled.

"I have indeed, oh mighty commander," Faart replied, pointing to a spot on the seat. "But, I wouldn't use the throne for a short while, master. The fangs that once belonged to the vampire queen of Carmilla Prime are particularly sharp and pointy today. I wouldn't want your highness to, er... puncture his importance, if you get my meaning!"

But Major Pain wasn't listening. Engrossed in whatever he was reading, he slumped down heavily onto his throne — right on top of the freshly extended teeth. There was a brief pause, and then his eyes flashed yellow and he screamed.

Bigg, Smellie and the two children instantly fell about laughing, and even Faart allowed himself a small smile.

"I did try to warn him," he said with a shrug. "But that still doesn't solve our problem. If we don't conquer Earth in the name of Soolin within one turn of your world, Major Pain will throw us all into the Dungeon of Dirtiepants!"

Smellie shuddered.

Megan squinted at the glass tablet. "Does that thing record video as well as show it?"

"It does indeed," said Bigg with a nod. "It can broadcast live, too."

A smile spread across Megan's face. "Then I've got an idea..."

# CHAPTER FOUR
## Interruption

The villagers gathered in the Badger's Bottom town hall. "And I say we should ban beef crisps! They are taking customers away from my butcher's shop. And they always repeat on you."

The overweight man in the long white coat pushed his hands into his pockets and looked sternly at other shop owners.

"Mr Eggs," said an elderly woman with golden blonde hair, "may I remind you that we're not here to discuss the crisps in my sweet shop," said Penny Mix. "Perhaps you can tell us why you have called the meeting, Hammond?"

"What are you talking about? I didn't call this meeting!" said Hammond Eggs.

"Neither did I," said Daisy Roots. "I should be back at the shop. I have flowers to deliver."

"Well, someone must have left those messages!" said Penny Mix.

"Not me," stated Reverend Neil Down. "Gerupta, how about you?"

"Don't look at me," replied Mr Singh. "I've got music lessons to prepare for when school starts again."

Doctor Koff coughed, "Then, who did summon us all here?"

"We did!" cried two voices from the back of the hall.

The assembled folk of Badger's Bottom turned to see Jamie and Megan approaching

— along with three small creatures with grey skin and huge heads.

"Aliens!" screamed Daisy. Then she dropped to the floor, out cold. Doctor Koff dashed over to kneel beside her.

Faart looked up at the children. "Remember when I asked you to take us to your leader? Is this really the best you can do?"

Jamie nodded. "This is the parish council. The only leaders we've got access to. Sorry."

"What, no money-grabbing president? What about a deviously cunning evil overlord?"

"Oh, we've got them!" said Jamie. "But they're too busy running the banks. Plus, we don't have time to go and see them, I'm afraid. The council of Badger's Bottom will have to do."

"It's all right," said Doctor Koff, grabbing

a cushion from one of the chairs and putting it under Daisy Roots's head. "She's just fainted."

"I'm not surprised!" thundered Mr Eggs, scowling at the new arrivals. "We have evil aliens in our midst. Children, step away from the extra-terrestrials."

"No, it's OK," insisted Megan. "They're not here to do us any harm."

Smellie cleared his throat. "Well, technically, we are..."

"We're here to invade your planet!" squeaked Faart, excitedly.

This time, it was Reverend Down's turn to faint. Mr Singh went to look after him.

"What's wrong with the adults in your world?" Bigg said. "Do they all behave like this when faced with unexpected arrivals from a galaxy far, far away?"

Jamie shrugged. "Pretty much."

Mr Eggs growled under his breath and raised his fists. "If you monsters want this world, you'll have to come through me first!"

Mrs Mix rested a hand on his shoulder. "Calm down, Hammond!" she commanded. "If Jamie and Megan aren't scared of our visitors, then we shouldn't be either."

"Penny's got a point," agreed Doctor Koff.

Penny Mix smiled kindly and approached

the children and their alien friends.

"Now," she said, sitting in the chair nearest to them. "Why don't we have a cup of tea, and you can explain exactly what is going on."

Half an hour later, Hammond Eggs locked the door to the village hall. "Right!" he said firmly. "We all know what we have to do?"

"I think so," replied Mr Singh. "And we're definitely meeting up at Jamie's house just before sunset."

"Exactly!" said Daisy Roots.

"Then it's all arranged," said Penny Mix. "Let's go and prepare for the end of the world!"

# CHAPTER FIVE
## Idea

On Planet Soolin, the door at the back of the throne room burst open, and Major Pain strode in, wafting his hand in the air.

"I'd give that ten minutes if I were you, Faart," he said, scowling. "Faart? FAART? Where in the name of all things small and disgusting are you?"

His only answer was the silence.

"Oh, yes..." said Pain, easing himself gingerly down onto the seat of his throne.

"He's off invading that weird green and blue world, whatever it's called... Girth or Smurf, or something like that. I'd better check in and see how he and that rotten rabble are getting on."

The alien overlord tapped a few commands onto the surface his tablet, and a live video feed sprang into life. Then, Major Pain's chin almost hit the floor. On the screen was one of the most bloodthirsty battles he had ever witnessed.

The air was filled with smoke, powerful orchestral music rang out and the ruins of the city in the background was in flames.

Faart, armed with some kind of large weapon, strode into view, crushing entire

trees beneath his feet. Those humans he'd
researched before leaving must be tiny
in comparison to Soolin warriors! In the
background, a white-coated human doctor
ran back and forth treating the blood-
soaked wounded.

Suddenly, there was an UN! UN! UN! UN!
UN! sound, and the sky was filled with dozens
of flying saucers. They looked to be smaller
and less advanced than Soolin ships, but

Major Pain was in no doubt that this was how the people of Earth — that's the name of the pesky planet — were going to fight back.

Smellie appeared and, with a snarl, he turned and fired his own weapon at one of the ships. A jet of liquid shot out, covering the advancing spacecraft. Within seconds, the ship's hull began to melt! What new type of weapon had his Soolin soldiers developed?

The Major jumped up, no longer able to sit still in the presence of such horrible violence. He stared at his screen in disgust as Smellie marched over to where the remains of the ships lay. He then scooped up a handful of the wreckage, stuffed it into his mouth and began to eat!

Major Pain quickly clutched at his stomach. Just what kind of crazed warriors had he unleashed on this poor, unsuspecting planet? Something must have happened during the journey — these new Soolin soldiers were animals!

Back on Earth, Smellie grinned wickedly as he licked the remnants of the spaceship powder from his fingertips. Then, off to the far side of Jamie's garden, Megan gestured for Smellie to leave the scene. Glancing over to where Mr Singh was holding the glass tablet and filming the action, he ran out of the shot ... and launched into an almighty coughing fit!

"What's wrong, Smellie?" asked Megan, stooping to pat him on the back.

"It's that white stuff!" Smellie wheezed. "What did you call it? The stuff from inside the flying saucers? Sherbet! It's gone right up my nose!"

Megan passed the alien gardener a bottle

of water. "Flying saucers! My favourites!" she said, looking over to where Penny Mix was waving two rods in the air. Tied to the rods by lengths of thread were six flying saucer sweets. "Bigg's coloured water did a

really good job of dissolving the rice paper on the outside, especially when fired from one of our super soakers."

"Are you sure this meat stuff looks like whatever's inside you humans?" beamed Bigg as he showed Megan the mixture of mince and tomato ketchup.

Megan nodded. "Close enough to fool Major Pain, at least!" she grinned.

Mr Singh passed the tablet to Hammond Eggs, so he could conduct the school band. They began playing the dramatic music Mr Singh had written, almost drowning out the audio from Jamie's Space Invaders game.

Doctor Koff gave the scene another blast from the village hall's smoke machine.

This was the cue for Jamie to stagger across the performance area. He had ketchup sprayed all over him, and he cried out in pretend pain while pulling a long string of Mr Eggs's sausages through a hole in the front of his T-shirt.

Back on Planet Soolin, Major Pain threw up all over his throne.

# CHAPTER SIX
# Incoming!

Faart stomped off screen, smashing the last few bonsai trees beneath his feet.

"Careful!" hissed Smellie. "It took ages to plant those! And they're not cheap."

"Everything is being paid for out of the council emergency fund," said Reverend Down. "Apart from your city painting, Megan. I'd like to buy that, if I may?"

Megan looked surprised. "Even now I've set fire to it?"

"Especially now," grinned the vicar. "I can use it to illustrate this Sunday's sermon."

Doctor Koff appeared, dropping the dolls he had bandaged back into the box they had borrowed from the playgroup. "Going well, isn't it?"

Jamie wiped the ketchup from his face. "I think so," he said. "Do you reckon Major Pain is still watching?"

From where he was holding the tablet, Hammond gave a thumbs up. "According to this thing, he's still online!" he mouthed. "And there's a message coming through..."

"This is it!" beamed Megan to the three aliens. "Good luck guys!"

Bigg, Smellie and Faart stepped in front of the camera to see a very pale-looking Major Pain on the glass tablet.

"Ah! There you are!" their commander croaked. "W-well done, you three. Another glorious — if gory — victory for the S-Soolin empire."

"Thank you, your darkness," said Faart. "I guess we'll be on our way home again…"

"NO!" cried Major Pain. "I mean … don't hurry back. Stay there for a few years. Enslave the human race. Have a bit of fun. Just don't come back here soon!"

"Whatever you think is best," said Faart. Then, the screen went blank.

Major Pain dropped his tablet into its charging slot and tried to slow his breathing. That was close! If he hadn't played it quite so calmly, those three monsters might have come back to Soolin. And who knows what they would do once they got back? Take over, probably.

Relieved, Major Pain wiped his damp

brow with the back of his hand, then slumped down onto his throne — right on top of the vampire queen's fangs again.

"YEEEEEEEEEAAAAARRRGGGGHHHH!"

Back on Earth, Smellie shared a high-three with Bigg. "Looks like we're getting an extended holiday after all!" the gardener said with a grin.